CCep

Beautiful Griselda

A Story by Isol

Translated by Elisa Amado

Groundwood Books / House of Anansi Press

Toronto Berkeley

Princess Griselda was so
beautiful that almost
everyone she met fell head over
heels in love with her.

And that's not just a saying.

At court balls, the heads of princes and Knights rolled along behind her, sighing...

Beautiful!

just because they'd looked at her.

Griselda found this amusing.

Maybe because she was bored, or maybe just because they were at hand, Griselda soon began a head collection.

She varnished the crowned heads herself and classified them by region and hair color. Then she exhibited them like trophies in her golden chamber.

And in order to keep her collection growing,
Griselda worked hard every day to become
even more beautiful and perfect.

Baths in cold spring water every morning

Juice from sour fruit specially
brought from Tasmania

Removal of
any stray hair

Scales sung in
three octaves for
an hour a day

Stretching
and balancing
in crystal shoes

Griselda would look at herself in the mirror and feel happy. She liked it that people throughout the kingdom talked about her beauty.

But the truth was
that instead of loving
her, people feared her.

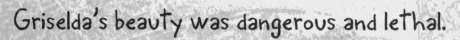
Griselda's beauty was dangerous and lethal.

The surrounding kingdoms
were slowly becoming headless,
as they lost most of their best kings and princes.

Nobody could resist Griselda,
so they began to hide from her.

Wherever she went,
doors and windows slammed shut
in a frightened hurry.

People stopped inviting her to balls,
coronations or anything.
"They're just jealous!" thought Griselda.

But eventually, the princess began to grow bored,
all alone in her palace surrounded by heads.

She wanted company.
Her servants avoided looking at her
for fear of losing their heads.
And even though her little dog was adorable,
she didn't have much in common with him.

So Griselda invited the most shortsighted prince in her county for dinner. His myopia allowed the prince's head to remain on his shoulders for several hours, until he finally perceived the princess's beauty...

with the usual result.

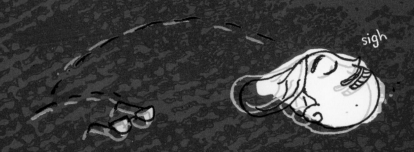

sigh

This princely romance had been brief,

but it left its mark on her.

Nine months later, Griselda had a baby girl who looked a lot like her.

"How beautiful!" she exclaimed.

That was the day she lost her head.

The baby princess
didn't find this at all amusing.

"Can't you fix it?"
she seemed to say.
But nobody knew how...

nor did they really feel like trying.

Fortunately, the baby princess
soon amused herself doing other things.

Everyone wanted to get to know her
and play with her.

The baby had the gift of charm,
and the palace was soon filled with laughter.

In time, she learned to draw, tell stories,
put on plays and even read maps...

But her favorite toys were jigsaw puzzles.
She loved putting things back together.

THE END

Groundwood Books / House of Anansi Press
110 Spadina Avenue, Suite 801, Toronto, Ontario M5V 2K4
or c/o Publishers Group West
1700 Fourth Street, Berkeley, CA 94710

We acknowledge for their financial support of our publishing program the Government of Canada through the Canada Book Fund (CBF).

Library and Archives Canada Cataloguing in Publication

Isol
Beautiful Griselda / written and illustrated by Isol ; translated by Elisa Amado.

Translation of: La bella Griselda.
ISBN 978-1-55498-105-2

I. Amado, Elisa II. Title.

PZ7.I838413Be 2011   j863'.64   C2011-902088-2

The illustrations were done in pencil, oil pastel and collage, then processed on the computer using four Pantone colors.
Printed and bound in China

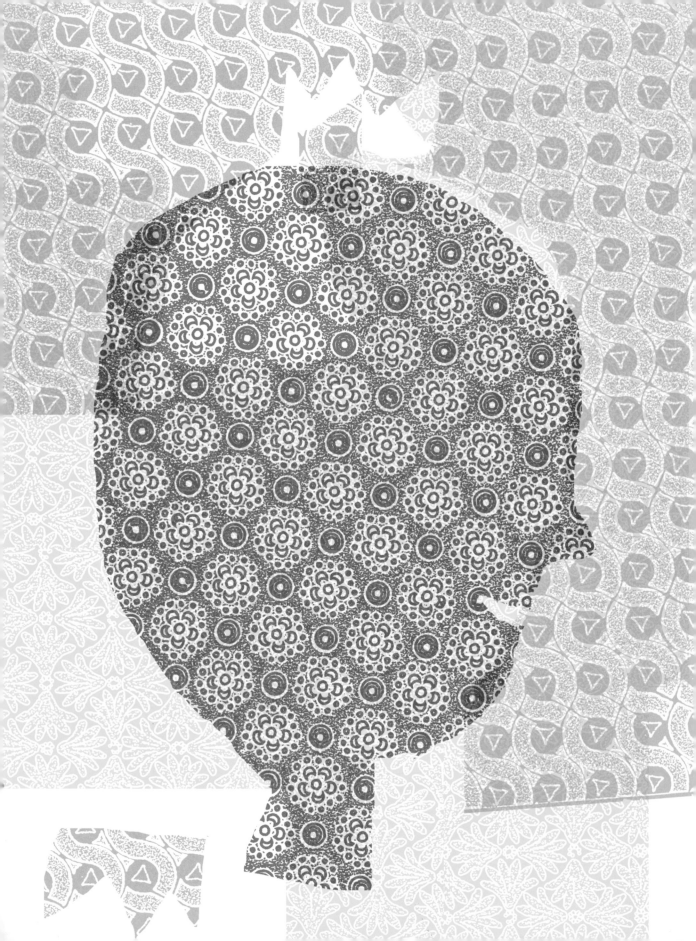